Note to Parents

Animal Antics, Level 1 of the *Now I'm Reading!*™ series, uses a step-by-step approach to introduce the emergent reader to the beginning phonics skills of short-vowel sounds.

Each of these five fun-filled stories will make your child giggle with delight as he or she practices each short-vowel sound. At the same time, other basic reading skills, such as sight words, consonants, word endings, digraphs, and consonant blends, will be reinforced. Story 1 is the easiest and story 5 is the most challenging. For optimum success, have your child read the stories in sequence the first few times. After that, as your child grows more comfortable with the various skills, he or she can read the stories in any order.

For more information on how to use these stories with your child, refer to the pages at the end of this book.

NOW I'M READING!™

ANIMAL ANTICS

LEVEL 1 ■ VOLUME 2

Written by Nora Gaydos
Illustrated by BB Sams

Table of Contents

CRAB
TRAP

Skills in this story: Vowel sound: short *a*; Sight words: *the, and, on, a, is*;
Word ending: *-s*; Initial consonant blends: *cr, gr, tr, sn*

■ ■ ■ ■ ■ ■ ■ ■ ■ ■ ■ ■ ■ ■ ■ ■ ■ ■ ■ ■

The crab.

The bad crab.

The bad crab grabs.

The bad crab grabs ham.

The bad crab grabs ham and jam.

The bad crab dabs
ham and jam on a trap.

BAM! WHAM!

The trap snaps.

The crab nabs a rat.

The rat is mad.

■ STORY 2 ■

FROG COPS

Skills in this story: Vowel sound: short *o;* Sight words: *the, with, by, in, up;*
Word ending: *-s;* Initial consonant blends: *fr, sp, dr, tr;* Final consonant blend: *-nd;*
Initial consonant digraph: *-sh*

■ ■ ■ ■ ■ ■ ■ ■ ■ ■ ■ ■ ■ ■ ■ ■ ■ ■ ■

The frog.

The frog with spots.

The frog with spots robs.

The frog with spots robs the shop.

The frog with spots
robs the mop shop.

The frog with spots
robs the mop shop by the pond.

KNOCK, KNOCK!

The frog with spots
drops the mops.

The frog cops trot in the shop.

The frog cops lock up the frog with spots.

■ STORY 3 ■

FISH

GIFT

Skills in this story: Vowel sound: short *i*; Sight words: *the, with, its, it, is, a*; Word ending: *-s*; Initial consonant blends: *sn, dr, sp*; Final consonant blend: *-ft*; Final consonant digraph: *-sh*

■ ■

The fish.

The fish lifts.

The fish lifts the gift.

The fish lifts the gift with its fins.

SNIP, SNIP!

The fish rips the gift.

It is a bib.

The bib fits the fish.

Drip, drip, spill!

The gift is a hit.

STUCK
DUCK!

Skills in this story: Vowel sound: short *u*; Sight words: *the, is, on, a, with;*
Word ending: *-s;* Initial consonant blends: *pl, st, tr, sk;* Final consonant blend: *-mp, -nk*

The duck.

The plump duck.

The plump duck is stuck.

The plump duck is stuck on a truck.

The plump duck is stuck
on a dump truck.

The plump duck is stuck
on a dump truck with junk.

JUMP, DUCK, JUMP!

Bum luck!

The plump duck jumps on a skunk.

The plump duck stunk!

ELK

YELPS!

:ills in this story: Vowel sound: short *e;* Sight words: *the, on, a, to, off, is, for;*
rd ending: *-s;* Initial consonant blends: *sl, sp;* Final consonant blends: *-lk, -xt, -nt, -lp*

■ ■

The elk.

The elk fell.

The elk fell on a sled.

The elk fell on a sled
next to a deck.

YELP, YELP!

The sled sped.

The elk on the sled sped
off the deck.

The sled gets a dent.

The elk is a mess.

The elk yells for help!

How to Use This Book

Prepare by reading the stories ahead of time.
Familiarize yourself with the skills reinforced in each
story. By doing this, you can better guide your child in
recognizing the new words and sounds as they appear in
the text.

Before reading, look at the pictures with your child.
Encourage him or her to tell the story through the pictures.
Next, read the books aloud to your child. Point to the
words as you read to promote a connection between the
spoken word and the printed word.

Have your child read to you. Encourage him or her to
point to the words as he or she reads. By doing so, your
child will begin to understand that each word has a
separate sound and is represented in a distinct way
on the page.

Encourage your child to read independently. This is
the ultimate goal. Have him or her read alone or read
aloud to other family members and friends.

■ ■ ■ After You Read Activities ■ ■ ■ ■

To help reinforce comprehension of the story:
- Ask your child simple questions about the characters, such as "What does the crab grab?" (from *Crab Trap*).
- Ask questions that require an understanding of the story, such as "Why is the rat mad?"

To reinforce phonetic vowel sounds:
- Ask your child to say words that rhyme with each other and have the same short-vowel sound. For example, *crab*, *grab*, and *lab*.

To reinforce understanding of words:
- Pick out two or three words from the story and have your child use all of them in a sentence.

To help develop imagination:
- Ask your child to make up a story, using his or her favorite characters from the book.
- Write the story down so your child can read his or her story later on.
- Have your child draw pictures to go with the story.

■ ■ ■ The Now I'm Reading!™ Series ■ ■

The *Now I'm Reading!*™ series integrates the best of phonics and literature-based reading. Phonics emphasizes letter-sound relationships, while a literature-based approach brings the enjoyment and excitement of a real story. The series has six reading levels:

Pre-Reader: Children "read" simple, patterned, and repetitive text and use picture clues to help them along.

Level 1: Children learn short vowel sounds, simple consonant sounds, and common sight words.

Level 2: Children learn long and short vowel sounds, more consonants and consonant blends, plus more sight word reinforcement.

Level 3: Children learn new vowel sounds, with more consonant blends, double consonants, and longer words and sentences.

Level 4: Children learn advanced word skills, including silent letters, multi-syllable words, compound words, and contractions.

Independent: Children are introduced to high-interest topics as they tackle challenging vocabulary words and information by using previous phonics skills.

Glossary of Terms

Phonics: The use of letter-sound relationships to help youngsters identify written words.

Sight Words: Frequently used words, recognized automatically on sight, which do not require decoding, such as *a, the, is,* and so on.

Decoding: Breaking a word into parts, giving each letter or letter combination its corresponding sound, and then pronouncing the word (sometimes called "sounding out").

Consonant Letters: Letters that represent the consonant sounds and, except *Y,* are not vowels—*B, C, D, F, G, H, J, K, L, M, N, P, Q, R, S, T, V, W, X, Y, Z.*

Short Vowels: The vowel sounds similar to the sound of *a* in *cat, o* in *dog, i* in *pig, u* in *cub,* and *e* in *hen.*

Long Vowels: The vowel sounds that are the same as the names of the alphabet letters *a, e, i, o,* and *u.* Except for *y,* long-vowel words have two vowels in them. They either have a silent *e* at the end of the word (for example *home*), or they use a vowel pattern or combination, such as *ai, ee, ea, oa, ue,* and so on.

Consonant Blend: A sequence of two or more consonants in a word, each of which holds its distinct sound when the word is pronounced. Consonant blends can occur at the beginning or at the end of a word—as in *slip* or *last* or *street.*

Consonant Digraph: A combination of two consonant letters that represent a single speech sound, which is different from either consonant sound alone. Consonant digraphs can occur at the beginning or the end of a word—as in *ship* or *fish.*

Literature-Based Reading: Using quality stories and books to help children learn to read.

Reading Comprehension: The ability to understand and integrate information from the text that is read. The skill ranges from a literal understanding of a text to a more critical and creative appreciation of it.

About the Author

Nora Gaydos is an elementary school teacher with more than ten years of classroom experience teaching kindergarten, first grade, and third grade. She has a broad understanding of how beginning readers develop from the earliest stage of pre-reading to becoming independent, self-motivated readers. Nora has a degree in elementary education from Miami University in Ohio and lives in Connecticut with her husband and two sons. Nora is also the author of *Now I Know My ABCs* and *Now I Know My 1, 2, 3's*, as well as other early-learning concept books published by innovativeKids®.

Damaged note 10 / 13 / 08
pages wrinkled VI